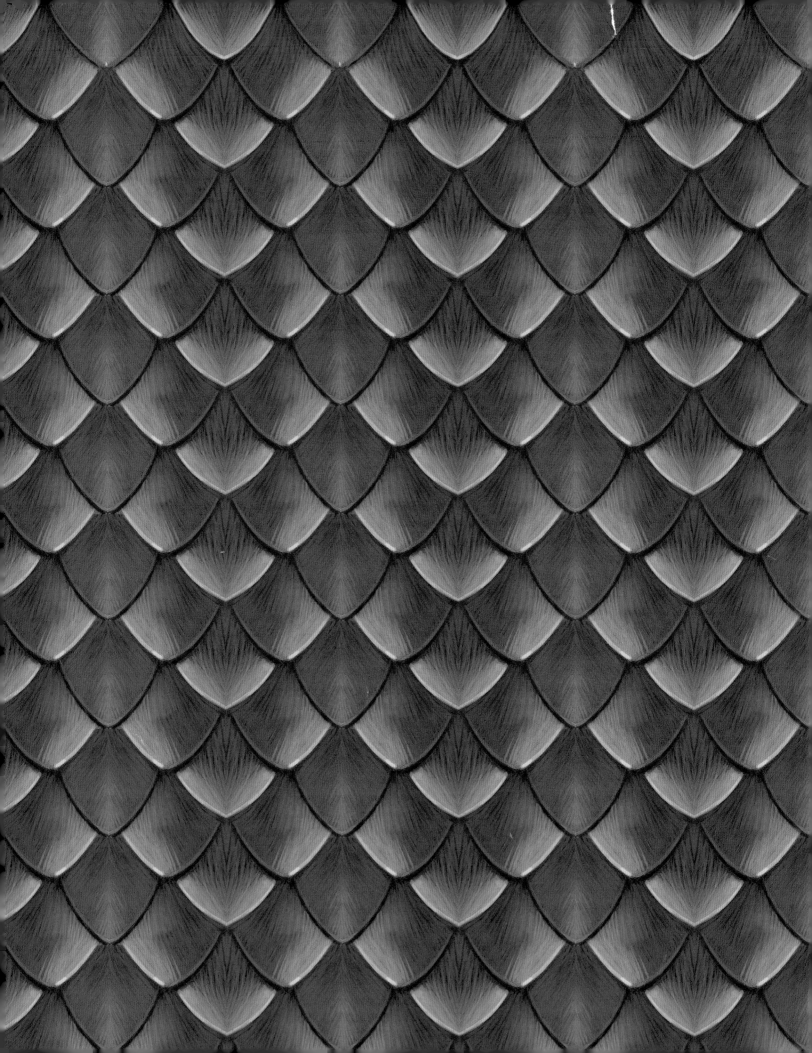

My Little Pony

The Dragons on Dazzle Island

Mary Jane Begin

Little, Brown and Company

New York • Boston

Little, Brown and Company

Hachette Book Group
1290 Avenue of the Americas, New York, NY 10104
Visit us at lb-kids.com

Little, Brown and Company is a division of Hachette Book Group, Inc.
The Little, Brown name and logo are trademarks of Hachette Book Group, Inc.

The publisher is not responsible for websites (or their content) that are not owned by the publisher.

First Edition: September 2016

Library of Congress Cataloging-in-Publication Data
Names: Begin, Mary Jane, author.
Title: The dragons on Dazzle Island / by Mary Jane Begin.
Description: First ed. | New York ; Boston : Little, Brown and Company, 2016. | Series: My little pony | Summary: "Twilight Sparkle and her friends are called to a remote island where the gem mine has been invaded by a flock of dragons laying their eggs! The ponies must use their power of friendship to save the day!"—Provided by publisher.
Identifiers: LCCN 2015037233 | ISBN 9780316282277 (hc) | ISBN 9780316282260 (ebook)
Classification: LCC PZ7.B388216 Dr 2016 | DDC (E)—dc22
LC record available at http://lccn.loc.gov/2015037233

10 9 8 7 6 5 4 3 2 1

APS

Printed in China

To Tim,
the love of my life

One morning, Rarity receives an upsetting letter. *"Noooo!"* she exclaims. "My *entire* order of rare island gemstones is canceled. My fall fashion line for Canterlot Carousel will be ruined! Of all the worst things that could happen, this is the *worst possible thing*!"

Rarity bursts into the Castle of Friendship with tears in her eyes and hands the letter to her friends.

Rainbow Dash reads it aloud. "'The Great Dragon Migration has brought dragons to Dazzle Island. Nopony can gather gems until they leave.'"

"Maybe the dragons are waiting for their welcome party!" says Pinkie Pie.

"Fluttershy could fly out there and give those dragons *The Stare*," says Applejack.

"Oh, I couldn't do that to a bunch of dragons who aren't hurting anypony," says Fluttershy, "but maybe *somepony* can explain to them why they need to move."

"Or some *dragon*," says Spike. He turns to Princess Twilight Sparkle. "I'm a dragon; they're dragons. Let me do this for Rarity."

The next day, Spike and Fluttershy sail toward Dazzle Island in the *Windhorse*. As they get closer, the clear blue sky turns steely gray and whipping winds toss the ship about. It's bumpy, but they're finally able to land. Fluttershy and Spike are confused by their new environment—for a tropical island, it's cold!

"This island looked warmer and sparklier in Twilight's books. Either the Pegasus ponies made a mistake with the weather or this is the work of—"

"Windigos!" says an approaching Island pony. "The winter spirits that feed on fighting might be here to stay if the dragons don't leave. We have had enough! Hi, I'm Blue Topaz."

"I'm Spike, and this is my friend Fluttershy. We came here to help so you can get back to harvesting those delicious—I mean, rare—gems. Can you bring us to the dragons?"

The colt brings the visitors to the dragons. He and Fluttershy watch as Spike tries to reason with a fellow dragon.

"Hey there, I'm Spike. Can we talk, just the two of us, dragon to dragon? See, I have a friend named Rarity—you might have heard of her..."

"...Rarity, the most beautiful and talented pony in Ponyville—maybe even in all of Equestria! Well, except for the princess. And the other princesses. Anyway, she really needs those gems you've got under your big, sharp claws and pointy tail. Rarity—"

Suddenly, the dragon blows Spike away with one smoky puff.

"Spike!" shrieks Fluttershy.

Seeing that her friend is okay, Fluttershy turns to face the dragon.
"Excuse me, but where I'm from, we show kindness to visitors."
With a heavy sigh, the enormous dragon stands up and moves.
"Spike! Look at this!" says Fluttershy. "These dragons are
mommies. They are just protecting their dragon eggs!"

An island filly named Ruby Redheart approaches the visitors. "You're right. I've been watching the dragons very closely. I don't think the dragons will leave until their babies hatch...and they'll never hatch unless this deep freeze ends!"

The Windigos fill the sky as the ponies and dragons continue to quarrel.

"When I was just a dragon egg, Princess Twilight hatched me. I wonder if there's a way to hatch these eggs without magic," says Spike.

"Well, I don't know if it's magic, but when I hug an egg with all my heart," begins Ruby Redheart, "the eggs and the gems start to—"

"Glow!" cry Spike and Fluttershy together.

"I think this could help warm the eggs so they can hatch!" cries Ruby.

Fluttershy turns again to the dragon. "When your eggs hatch, will you leave this island with your babies? Will you let us help you?" she asks.

The dragon nods.

As Ruby hugs the egg, Spike notices that the winds calm down and the frost begins to melt. He dashes off to the village and calls for help.

"Once upon a time, a very special pony helped hatch me. If we each hug an egg, we can warm it and help the baby dragon inside hatch. The dragons need you and everypony who has a heart!"

Soon Spike leads a parade of townsponies into the valley. Fluttershy shows the crowd how to wrap their hooves around the eggs with love. Although it's cold, everypony hugs and hugs their dragon eggs through the night, hoping to warm the babies inside.

More and more ponies hug the dragon eggs.
No longer fed by anger and misunderstanding, the
Windigos lose their strength and disappear, restoring
warmth to the island.

"It's working!" Ruby cries as one baby dragon
after another is born.

When the last baby is born and the dragons prepare to leave, Blue Topaz lets them know that they are welcome to migrate to the island and share their gems anytime.

"I promise to help hatch the babies when you do come back!" says Ruby.

Just then, Ruby Redheart's cutie mark—a tiny dragon egg—appears on her flank.

"Thanks for all your help," call Blue Topaz and Ruby
Redheart as they wave good-bye to their new friends.
Fluttershy and Spike know that it will be smooth sailing
back to Ponyville now that the Windigos are gone.

"The Magic of Friendship has come to the rescue again. Your gems are on the way, Rarity!" says Spike.

Fluttershy adds, "We met a kind filly named Ruby Redheart, who got her cutie mark in dragon care...and we helped so many cute baby dragons!"

"I bet they were cute...but I bet none were as cute as our Spike," says Rarity with a wink.

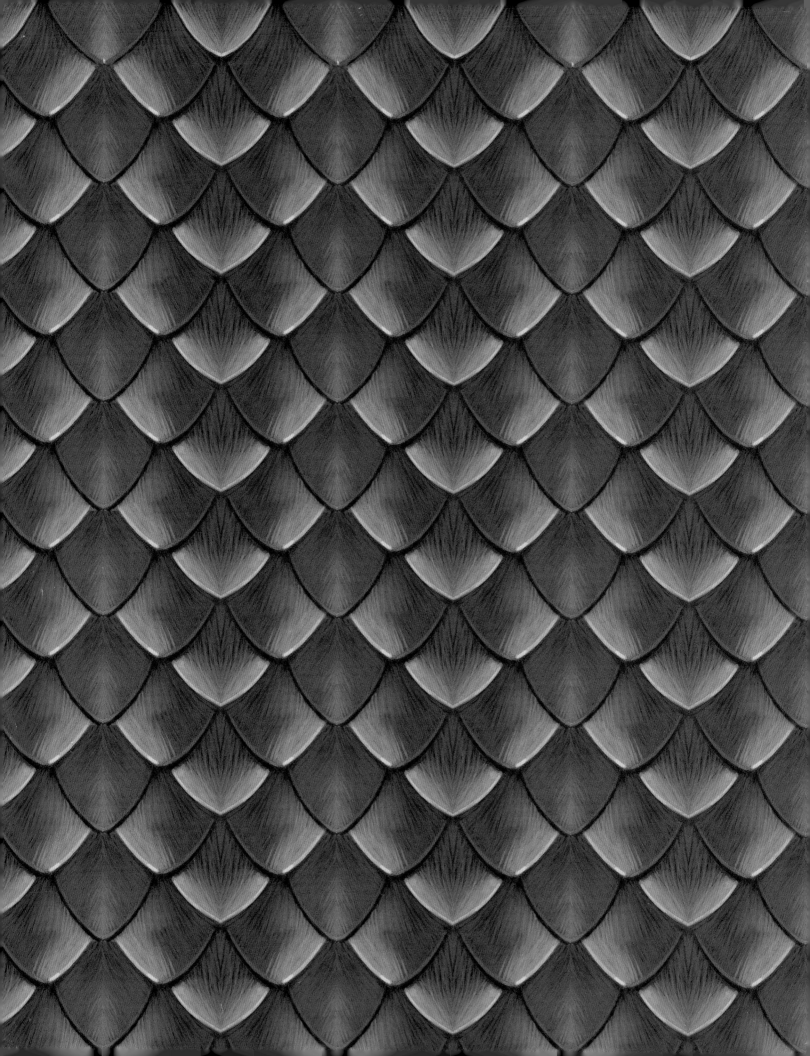